BIG WORDS FOR LITTLE PEOPLE

Helen Mortimer & Cristina Trapanese

Our World

MUSEUM

Share

We all share our planet. We are one global family.

WELCOME TO OUR WORLD

Past and future

The world has an amazing history.

Why did the dinosaurs die out?

A stone age invention!

Learning from the past helps us think about what we can do for a brighter future.

Wild

Wild places are precious and so are the plants, animals and people that live in them.

Save

We get water and energy from our planet but we should do what we can to save our resources and not waste them.

Reuse! Reduce! Recycle!

Danger

Nature can sometimes be dangerous.

My volcano is erupting!

But humans can also place nature in danger.

BAMBOO FORESTS ARE BEING CUT DOWN

What will the pandas eat?

Change

Our actions are important. We can take small steps to make big changes that protect the planet . . .

. . . and really make a difference!

Wonder

The world is full of wonder. From the bottom of the ocean . . . to the stars in the sky.

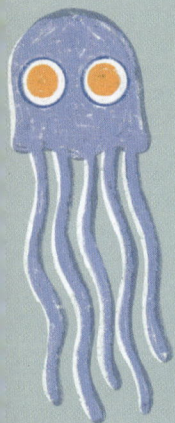

Fairness

Around the world people's lives can be very different. What should everyone have?

A home?

FOOD

SCHOOL

CLEAN WATER

HEALTH CARE

Peace and freedom

Peace begins with each of us. A better world is one where we all live free from fear and harm.

Belong

We should all feel that we
belong somewhere . . .
a place we can call home.

Be curious

Being curious about the world
opens our eyes so that we can see
the good things to celebrate
and the problems that
need solving.

Our world

Every one of us is part of our world. It is ours to understand, enjoy and look after.

RECYCLE!

Save
the
WHALE!

I LOVE
TREES!

BE KIND TO
EACH OTHER!

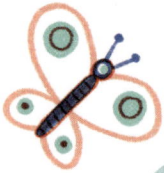

Ten ideas for getting the most from this book

1 Take your time. Sharing a book gives you a precious chance to experience something together and provides so many things to talk about.

2 This book is all about our world: how we live in it and how we can look after it. What small step could you take to help the planet today?

3 It's also a book about language. Ask each other what three words you would use to describe the world we live in and three words to describe your hopes for the planet.

4 The illustrations in this book capture various moments on a visit to a musuem. We've intentionally not given the children names – so that you can choose your own and perhaps invent something about their personalities.

5 If you were visiting the museum in this book what would be your favourite gallery or display?

6 Talk about what the children might learn from their museum trip. How has it helped them to understand the world?

7 Why not make a colourful poster to explain one of the global themes that are explored in the museum? You could add some words that help us think about the topic.

SAVE

8 By recognizing how amazing our world is and the challenges that it faces, we hope this book will help readers develop into responsible global citizens.

9 Live local, think global! There is probably a museum not far from where you live. Perhaps this book will inspire you to visit it together.

10 You could each choose a favourite word about our world from the book – it will probably be different each time you share the story!

Glossary

global – something which is global is to do with the whole world

green – if we are green, we behave in a way which is good for the environment

harm – damage or injury

protect – if we protect something, we look after it so it is kept safe

resources – the planet's natural resources include water, air, soil and animals